PANDEMIA

(2020 Vision)

JOSEPH MOCTEZUMA

BALBOA.PRESS
A DIVISION OF HAY HOUSE

Balboa Press books may be ordered through booksellers or by contacting:

Balboa Press
A Division of Hay House
1663 Liberty Drive
Bloomington, IN 47403
www.balboapress.com
844-682-1282

Because of the dynamic nature of the Internet, any web addresses or
links contained in this book may have changed since publication and
may no longer be valid. The views expressed in this work are solely those
of the author and do not necessarily reflect the views of the publisher,
and the publisher hereby disclaims any responsibility for them.

The author of this book does not dispense medical advice or prescribe
the use of any technique as a form of treatment for physical, emotional,
or medical problems without the advice of a physician, either directly
or indirectly. The intent of the author is only to offer information
of a general nature to help you in your quest for emotional and
spiritual well-being. In the event you use any of the information in
this book for yourself, which is your constitutional right, the author
and the publisher assume no responsibility for your actions.

Print information available on the last page.

ISBN: 978-1-9822-5629-6 (sc)
ISBN: 978-1-9822-5630-2 (e)

Balboa Press rev. date: 10/09/2020

Contents

PANDEMIA 1 1

Stanka 4

The Thornbird 15

The Response 19

Shania 22

Shania 24

My Italian Father 28

Paris! 30

The Idyllic Place Called Home 33

The War 37

The German Lockdown 40

Pandemic of the Mind 42

D Day 43

America 45

Cross Country; Route 66 49

California 51

Love Becomes Destiny 52

The Vision 54

The Mirror of the Mind 57

PANDEMIA 2 61

PANDEMIA 3 65

PANDEMIA 4 69

PANDEMIA 5 73

PANDEMIA 6 75

PANDEMIA 7 77

PANDEMIA 8 81

PANDEMIA 8.5 85

PANDEMIA 9 87

PANDEMIA 10 91

PANDEMIA 11 95

PANDEMIA 12 97

PANDEMIA 1

It was surreal, like wakening up into a dream and reality was no longer there. In this dream you lose everything that you would call ownership. Little by little, you lose control of everything. Everything loses its value: your diplomas that you so proud hanged on the wall. Your degrees and your achievement all lose their precious value. The money that you sacrificed all your life to save lose its gleerer and its shining content in your eyes. The friends and networks of people that you always connect yourself with. They become useless. Like a decoration that your mind use to hang on you to take away your loneliness.

You are left naked! In the middle of Broadway. All your strengths of the pillar and bastion that you were and gives you surety, was gone, like a simple dress that cover your soul. The predictable life that you use to have, vanished like smoke, leaving you in an unpredictable world leading nowhere an uncertain road, in an unknown universe unaware of you, making you be nothing by its indifference.

What happened? Did my mind changed and shift into another dimension? Could the mind shifts gears and go to a totally different reality? But the reality that we used to live and got so acquainted so, vanished before our eyes. Nothing is left but truces of our civilization culture and way of life.

All in one instant our way of life was torn to pieces. Yesterday disappeared before our eyes and now the present in an unknown that make each and every one nervous and unsure of how to deal with this new reality. The survival rate going from zero to ten or more. Each one become expendable, and were are place in a situation where a healer and doctor decides who lives und who dies.

Stanka

Stanka called from Bulgaria this morning. She woke me up saying; "what is going on over there in the United States? We are seeing all these riots going on, and it is so sad, very sad…"

I was thinking for an instant, she was talking about another country, but it was the country I lived for the last 60 years, she did not understand, being white and European, that there is an engrained culture in the U.S. allowing racism and prejudice to foment and breed more so virulent that the corona virus infesting our nation now.

There is a culture of colors, by color you are define your position in life. By color you are bestowed the merit of obtaining a schooling, a scholarship or a job... the one that are white will received a "white card" that is what a Italian friend convey in private one time. They thought he was white because of his skin color and he was giving the privilege to obtain a white card, so he can go to places only for whites.

Stanka, how is it over there in Bulgaria?

"It's beautiful, Joseph, it is all green this time of the year, I want you and Nellie to come and visit me, when this lockdown is over.

Nobody is dying over there of Coronavirus?

No, very few sick people over here, but you must come

How is your family?

All my son moved to Oregon, it is a safer place over there than in California, which life is very expensive.

Tell me about it, I lived in California all my life, yet I would not move to any place else, I love the sunshine and look at my backyard Stanka, full of flowers and roses, you should come and visit me, I promised we will have a good time.

When I recalled, I spend all my life in California. I realized that all that is happening now is a seasonal cycle of forever return: the new dragon rocket sending two astronauts to Space Station in orbit, reminds me of the landing on the moon, around 69 and the riots going on right now reminds me of the Watts riots in 64, 72, 92 etc., with the same grievances and complaints. The coronavirus pandemia reminds me of the flu epidemic in World War 1, not that I lived through that incident, but it is a historical memory of my history class.

Everything returns on this earth. Nothing is new under the sun, so there is nothing to be afraid of anymore. At least not for me.

I meet Stanka twenty years ago, when I wanted to do something more out of life; the sting with the state and me as a state employee came to an abrupt end. I wanted to fulfill a dream I had since I was 12 when I saw "To Sir with Love" with Sidney Poitier and fell that it was my calling to be a teacher.

I went back to school, obtain a master's degree, and started working for a college, when I saw Stanka for the first time.

She was an educator, but much more than that.

She help people advance in life by helping them as a counselor, friend or colleague.

I always thought she had mystical powers in the way she dealt with spiritual things and always engaging into dreams or projects that she concocted out of her mind and made then seem real. Her presentation was so real of her projects that I felt couple of time for it.

She came up with the idea that she met this young enterprising man from Bulgaria, that acquired a satellite or at least the rights of a satellite and wanted fill with content the 12 hours of transmission that was allocated to him. he made slots for different kind of programming, one of them was Mexican b movies the ones that were made for 25000 dollars made in couple of months.

And if I help him and her to obtain such movies and music (mariachi music) I could get 15 percent of the gross revenue, I was thrilled and knew at least my causing Leslie making movies in Hollywood.

I set my old van seating 7 ready to meet Leslie and her producer, a savvy, intelligent enterprising young man willing and able to do a deal with this millionaire from Bulgaria

I was the driver and it reminds me of Magical Mystery Tour that the Beatles did going on a trip not knowing what to expect in Hollywood, land of dreams and passions combined with broken rainbows on the ground after a rainy day.

I drove Stanka and her committee of seven driving to L.A. in a with expanse of land of freeways and speeding cars going on the crazy race of work and play.

It was my hometown. Los Angeles called my spirit and body to live in it long time ago, yet I could not figure out how its center was nowhere to be found because its center was nowhere, I guess that was also why I was nowhere man, like the Beatles song.

But it was the center of attraction for the whole world wanted to come here. I blame it on the pyramid on top of the City Hall that cause of such attraction. Who cares about the Pyramids of Egypt? We have our own pyramid of the mind and drfas here where the mind rules with Hollywood's dreams of glory and desires that turn into passions that ends in a tragic way on Ventura highway.

Buried in the sands of Pacific Coast Highways.

Nothing stands permanent here, not even your eyes, amazed at the edification of glory of downtown buildings.

We got out of the van and follow the footsteps of the grand terrace that lead to a conference room with 12 or more executive chairs, which swivels to our desire.

Damain appears a commanding presence in the middle of Bulgarian people and Latin beauties dress up as executive secretaries.

"What can I do for you?" he spoke with grave and elegant voice. Denoting that his time was precious.

Nobody has time in Hollywood, but for some mystery and strange reason more than a thousand movies are done by these same people out of time.

Stanka started introducing the entourage, I was presented as a writer, after Leslie introduced Damain to all of us, and the proposal was made.

Damain said: "I have all the B moves you required and move I can supply to your request.

After hour of discussion, can the finalized details of a possible contract. My hands were already sweaty of the emotion of the art of the deal…

One final piece of this contractual puzzle needed to see the completion of our dream, "how is this going to be pay?"

There was a dead silence in the room.

Stanka broke the silence and ice in the expression of everyone by saying with innocence an naivety that only a girl wondering at the world must have.

In order to start the project, Mr. Koshovo wanted me to ask you if you put the first 200,000. Dollars and he will pay you back as soon as he arrives at Las Vegas next week.

It seems that a balloon was deflated in the middle of our dreams. A pop goes the wisel suddenly awoken us of our little sleep by Stanka's magic.

Mr. Damein stood up and said in a quiet almost convicting voice: "no deal" thank you for coming and usher us to the door.

The deflated Magical Mystery group got into the van and Leslie said; "is anybody hungry? I am ready for lunch yeah, said Demetri, I buy you lunch.

This is how Stanka move hot air thru dreams that fly high as Zeppelins in the sky.

Just like magic.

It was Stanka's magic.

The Thornbird

The tragedy of this earth is that we are less than our dreams.

We are limited in so many aspects of our nature to receive the glory of ourselves.

We are trapped inside a needy world of wants and desires of passions and dreams that we will never reach, unobtainable to us.

We are less that our passions and they become lions and we are trapped inside a cave of hungry lions like Daniel and the den of lions.

Only God can save us from ourselves!

But before God saves us He placed the Holy Spirit to lead us into the desert of life; lack of opportunities, dead ends, and empty roads that does not lead to nowhere, yet in our hearts there is a home to reach, a port of call, a Chelsea refuge of an immense, uncertainty and mysterious sea, that losses our souls with the incoming waves of uncertainty, pandemic of fear and useless death.

Our souls are broken in this world, and we worked with a broken heart to do the impossible, we do miracles with a broken soul.

A broken symmetry we find in our quest to do right, the good, and find the beautiful and the truth of God and of ourselves.

We become a Thornbird, seeking without stopping, searching without finding, a wretched soul searching for one opportunity in life, for one shot to glory, one moment in the sunshine.

For broken souls like us, there is only one chance in life given to us that we can obtain glory.

The Thornbird flies high and low to find a thorn tree (a cross) and being mediocre in his song, and lousy singer, he knows that he only has one chance in his lifetime to sing like the angels of heaven, only once it is bestow upon him the glory of heavenly song, to confer upon him the song of heaven, yet it lies in that thorn tree (Calvary) to sing like heavens above.

But once he finds the tree and stand upon its branches, he finds the greater needle or spike to impaled himself on it and only then and solely then he can sing the most beautiful song on earth as well in heaven, while dying he sing only once in his lifetime the greatest song form him, while dying and an excruciating pain (the best part comes with the greatest pain).

The swan song of our existence is truly our perfection, and the end is only our beginning of glory amen.

The Response

I woke up and turn on the TV while I got up.

The plague was raising to level that turns reality to surrealism.

I didn't believe what I was living. Thousands of people dead, dropping dead like leaves from a tree or a fruit from the tree of life.

If life on this earth is like a tree. Than we are never safe, because the heavier our fruit in existence becomes, the more liable we are to be pick up by a bird (spirit) or drop off to the ground (six feet under).

The news cry out for the federal government to take over and organize on the national scale.

Pleading was torrent on all the 50 states, that this Republican president would bring his leadership to the national arena and to do what Roosevelt did in the 30's and 40's to championed a national respond to this crisis, empathy and sympathy from his libs to all those victims not of the virus, but his negligence and emcampedence of not knowing the gravity of the subject at hand; "let the states take care of this problem" The federal government is only for support".

What was needed was ppe and he let state bit on competing with each other profiteering the middle man on the expense of the victims.

I woke up naked, feeing useless for the first time in my life, thinking that I am just a geostatic person made only by all the activities which I perform on a daily basis; I am what I do, I am my action and my action is me, but today I feel incompetent because I fell I am constituted of so many actions of the past and today and now I am nothing for the new day.

Shania

FANTASTIC VOYAGE OF A LIFE TIME

I met this Russian Princess in this city of dreams instead of angels, for everything else are dominated by demons or to put is lightly by our demons, like they used to call them in the Renaissance age.

Hollywood is a city full of dreamers coming from all over the world. I was lucky to meet eastern European people like Stanka and my Russian Princess.

She said she knew me from another life, that we were lovers and had a fantastic voyage

thru time. SHE WANTED ME TO DO
HER LIFE IN A SCREENPLAY! Or be
her ghostwriter biographer, which I did.
But I want you to read her account in her
own writing with some ghost corrections
on the side.

Shania

I was born in Petrograd, Russia from Italian father and Polish mother. My father was a musician, he came to our country with a string Orchestra… on tour. One fortuitous night in a concert given by him, my mother and father met each other in a destiny embrace. They fell in love and married. My mother was 16 at the time.

The Northern climate of Russia was very harsh and cruel to people in love from other lands, especially for my dad, coming from a warm climate and native of Southern Italy, a place call Naples was detrimental to his health and succumb to the cold weather. He contorted pneumonia and being a heavy smoker since childhood die of Sarcoma when I was only two years old.

My mother had to work and took a job at the Red Cross as a nurse, and she sent me to my grandmother's. During this times, it was a bad period of history for Russia, just defeated in the German war, Russian was at the threshold of the Revolution. The situation got worse with rationing of food, and always living in constant fear of the ruthless, Godless Communists. The Red Army cut the country between North and South. My mother was in a hospital controlled by the White Army of General Wrangle, fighting the Reds in the South.

My mother met recuperating from his wounds, a young officer of the Aristocracy, a Baron by his ancestors from Vienna Austria, emigrated and settled in Russia. My mother attended his wounds and fell in love. It was the solace of love in the time of crises, they were lovers at wartime.

When the retreating army, or what was left of the remaining White Army was pushed all the way to Crimea. They retreated to Yalta at the Black Sea, there my mother married the already recuperated Baron and were evacuated to ConstantinopIa. My mother wanted so much to have me with her again, yet how? My mother and her husband managed to get to Paris on the Istanbul - Paris Express, luxury train, an elegant ride with Crystal Chandeliers, they stop at the lost outpost closest to Petrograd, they employed an Estonian lady to cross for them to the old town where I was with my grandmother, Estonia Tallinn, Ravel Town to look for me and take me to them, she came and took me breaking my Grandmother heart: my Babshka! Who died of grief and deprivation...

I never saw my Grandmother again......

My Italian Father

I was reunited with my mother and father, in fact, I only knew a father. By my birth I am Latin, Italian - registered in Italian Consulate from Consul in Revel. In fact, only one, that I really knew, besides some incidents in my childhood, when I was just over a year old, maybe close to two years old. I don't remember.

Only that - for my father, Italian, his Spaghetti was sacred: when the table was set, my mother and father sat down for dinner, I was sat in a high chair, father said to me in Italian, he always spoke to me in Italian: "Mango, Figlia Mia Mango." I refused- he insisted, so, I grabbed the table cloth and pulled it down to the floor with all of his beloved spaghetti!!!

It is hard to describe his rage, I could not sit down for three days - after being spanked. Other happier times, was when I was sitting on his shoulder, and he was walking on Nevsky Prospect in Petrograd to buy some toy at the Toy store for me. This is all that I remember of my biological father that gave me life.

Paris!

After Paris, nothing becomes important.
After Paris, everything else is a footnote.
After Paris, only remains the index of name and places.
After Paris, the remains of the day happens as an afterthought.
After Paris, it is only the night with dreams fulfilled.
After Paris, we can all go home.
After Paris, you can only enjoy a cigarette after good sex.
After Paris, all things are merely incidentals.
After Paris, is a soft flowing breeze in a sea of serene content.

After Paris we returned to Istanbul in the same luxury "train and live there for two years plus.

My first steps were on Turkish grounds, Turkish language - "Baksheesh"- "stood Jiis" - were the most used words.

Istanbul is a beautiful City- with its palaces with marble floors, minaret "Dolma Bacshi"- Haren, all that on the Bosphor River.

The city is divided by the bridge into two: European side and on the other side the natives. All the good shops and Cultures landmarks were on the European side. The Bridge was a toll bridge and you have to pay to pass!

My parents wanted to give me a good education, so we return to Paris. There was only French to speak, that was the language I excel and mastered. We live in Paris for eight years. Paris was Paris, many of bistros, and dunkers on the streets. An Eternal "Chanson de Came flour, Chanson d "Amour" accompanied with accordion player on the streets.

The Idyllic Place Called Home

Yet, that wasn't what my father wanted. He, being an aristocrat, was craving a royal court, but not in France, so we went to Royal Belgium. There we bought a small, but three stories high house in the most fashionable part of Brussels, located at the Avenue Louise, with its beautiful chestnut trees alley divided in three parts: the center for horseback, made of sand, and one on each side paved for autos, and wide sidewalks along the house.

The house had cellar for coal, which was deposit from an opening from the sidewalk.

They used coal for central heating, due to the fact that Belgium is a coal-mining country, coal was inexpensive for ordinary and high class people. There was also a wine cellar, food storage and a kitchen with three stoves. Coal, gas and electric refrigerator, freezer etc....

On the first floor of the house, there was an entrance or atrium for people or visitors to wait until the butler (with white gloves) would announce them to my father or my mother. Large, widening, red carpeted staircase, leading to the upstairs red sitting room with oriental tapestry on the walls, and all in red velvet furniture. Adjacent was a large dining room all in green velvet that could sit thirty people with the lift from the kitchen to serve food. Very convenient. There was an adjacent small wine room with electric refrigerator and small electric stove. There was a stairway, leading upstairs to the third floor to our mother, father and mine bedrooms, decorating in pink satin. Stairs up a studio for whatever business at hand.

The servant's quarters were three rooms for the cook, two maids and the butler. In Belgium, my education lasted years. At the age of 14, I was sent with one chaperon, and score of eleven girls my age to Florence, Italy to study the old Masters of the Renaissance and their manner and style of painting at the Gino Rossi, ancient art painting. I stay two years, traveling and going to see Eternal Rome and painted my Madonna (maternal love) a large painting 6x8 feet that after the death of my husband, I donated to Canyon City, Colorado Christian Church, Disciples of the Christ, in his memory. They venerated it very much, placing fresh flowers, on each church services. Coming back, I painted from the window of one house; Turkish Minaret, because it was a part of "Panorama of Cairo" in Exposition

Park. My education and studies encompasses Theology, Philosophy of Theosophy- I was seeking a religious Truth, a search for an Eternal Truth such as Almighty God!

At this time in Brussels, my life was "in an Ivory Tower" I was a princess- having servants, never washed a dish or cooked, even less not going to the kitchen –period. I was transported in a Buick Sedan with a Chauffeur. My activities were painting, going to exhibitions, dancing at balls and going to Ballet School. Then suddenly it happened, the world turn upside down.

The War

Then without warning, a reality has shift from Paradise:

Came the war, 1940, with the Germans occupation of Brussels... We decided to go, with the Belgian people in mass Exodus to France, trying to reach by the Northern sea side Normandy, then from there travel inside the country side to the town of Pau, very close to the Spanish Border, where our friend Countess Solaude Wickeer lee Edith was residing, nobody knew that it would be a nightmare.

The Exodus was impossible to describe: people walling with bird cages on their hands, on bicycles, rolls of cars with mattress on top, to protect against the low flying German planes with shotguns. "Mitroilleuses" were shooting people. People were carrying with them everything that they could save. We could not take in the car no one else, due to the fact that with us three, there was an elderly friend with her sick daughter, trying to reach her husband in the South of France, George Bia.

Finally with so many tragedies on the way we reach Pau and our friend with already one refugee at his home, Ambassador of Belgium. We stay for a few days, after father decided to go to Spain. So with a high paid guide, through the mountains by u small unknown road, we reached the Bridge on the River Irun, where the Spanish Border started.

To our surprise, the border was closed, we had to wait for three days until it open up, and once we arrive there, our disappointment was enormous when we found out that under French law, everything was supposed to be left in the border, before crossing: Everything! Money, valuables, jewelry, all possessions, even sugar that was already rationed in Pau. We convened that going to a foreign country not knowing the language without money; IMPOSSIBLE! We return home to Brussels.

The German Lockdown

We decided to return to already occupied Brussels by the German army, whereby they installed their headquarters across the street from our house. They tried to take over our home, but the smart housekeeper that we had, conveyed to them that the house was contaminated by deadly and strange disease which had be fallen our dear Baron. They let it go and instead took the mansion across the street from us.

The Resistance to the occupation was very strong, based on the belief that Belgians did not accept that easy defeat; they were sabotaging everything that would be useful to the Germans; water, roads, army wiring, etc....

Germans ordered no one on the streets after 10 at night. Curfew was imposed throughout the city. No cars, bicycles or other transportation permitted. From time to time, German Patrol would stop and search everyone in a car. Everyone would have a small knife in their pocket for self-defense and protection.

If the German would find out, they would be sent to the forced labor camps in Germany. Our car was stored in the garage and we anxiously waiting for liberation. Yet there was no news, and no radio was allowed to anyone.

Father was defying the ordinance, because he had one in the cellar, listening to the BBC of London, overcoming our fears, despite of the danger and risking to be sent to the Force Labor Camps in Germany.

Pandemic of the Mind

We were in quarantine, no one when out of his or her home. Months went by without news. The pandemic of our minds become real; no hope, no plans, no future for us was becoming evident with each and every day that passed.

What was of the past, was a ship that already left the port into a vast sea of uncertain future, with an undefined road in an ocean of unending blue waves, which brings to you nothing, and nothing in the horizon of our lives. Our liberty taken, imposed by forced the situation we now live.

D Day

D Day came and an awful retreat of the Germans from our city, wounded and dying on the streets, in front of our eyes, crying for help and no one would help them. Mostly young conscripts, pitiful to look at. At our door there was a dying German soldier, asking for water, but the Belgian Servitude refused to give him water. My mother could not stand for it… and gave him the water.

German high command left the mansion across the street and it was taken by the Allies, mostly American and took possession of it.

Father was giving a big reception to our liberators; English Colonel Villare and numerous American, among them. There were two brothers among the committee, Leonard and Howard Gorman, that became our constant friends and whose family became our sponsors to immigrate to America.

America

To emigrate to American was more difficult due to the fact there were "quotas" for every nationality. Fortunately these quotas were eliminated by President Kennedy, but we at that time 1945, had to wait three more years to 1948 for our quota, being that I was Italian and Russian.

Finally we sailed from Rottendam, on the New Amsterdam" a luxurious ship very similar to the "Queen Mary" that we could not take, because Father wanted his pet dogs (three of them) to go in our suite, and regulations on the Queen Mary required that they be put in a Kennel.

The "New Amsterdam" ship had two large Olympic size swimming pools, Gymnasium for any type of exercise, tennis court, a variety of hall games, a Ball Room, two dining rooms, theatre, night clubs, Bars, beauty shops, dress shops and gambling casino… indulgence on o grand scale.

To Cross the Atlantic took about seven days, usually five, but due to a ferocious storm in the high seas, we were delayed for three days more, not possible to reach, Hoboken, New York, earlier than that.

The Statue of Liberty welcome us to this marvelous new land, where freedom rings in every bell und hope build the dreams of people coming from far off lands, to breath the sense of progress and make their dreams reality.

When we were free to go from different inspections, we met our American friends from Syracuse, New York. We took a suite at the Governors' Clinton Hotel and on the 22th floor I met my fright. I was afraid of heights.

The suites had everything I could wish and desire: fruit, candy, flowers everywhere......
we went at chic nightclubs, the financial district of New York: Wall Street, where my Father transacted his monies deposited to his account from a Belgium Bank.

After spending one week at New York, we took a train to Syracuse, to meet our friends family and our sponsor to America, Mr. Gorman, we gave them gifts of every kind: we had many boxes of precious antiques, furs and other presents for them.

All our belongings were in storage in Hoboken, twelve huge crates, with antiques furniture and other miscellaneous items Gorman. Leonard and wife Mary offered their house to live for as long as we wanted. We lived at that time with their family: Olivia and Papa Gorman. We live there for a month, until a snowstorm arrived in Easter, which compel us to go to church with fur coats. It was not to father liking, so he purchased a Convertible Packard automobile with black upholstery and red leather, off the showroom, and we took off to California on route 66, which climate was similar to the Mediterranean Sea, back home in our French Nice.

Cross Country; Route 66

Along our long trip for u better climate, we were admiring different beauties along the way, changing with every State we crossed: Colorado "Mile High Bridge, deep black canyon, air became just like a fortifying drink, Arizona's mountains and "Painted Desert" which we admired from "El Tovar Hotel", Utah -Bryan Canyon with a sank Meteorite, unforgettable.

Kansas endless sea of green, endless fields that go into oblivion somewhere in the horizon. Texas red ground with orange red flowers. New Mexico, so picturesque with its fantastic, magical mountains. Finally California, the land of dreams and magical movies, Hollywood und the birth of flying. Natives say that in Spanish was called "Cali-fuerno" –Hot stove from San Bernardino to Pasadena, our destination is

"Paradise."

California

Orange and lemon groves all along the road welcome us, with an unforgettable, penetrating smell of the blossoming flowers, which surrender to your will. My father bought a hotel and stay in Pasadena when the agent sold to my Father the hotel Murphy.

Love Becomes Destiny

When the real estate agent who sold my father the hotel was given a party at my father's home, that when I met my destiny, I fall in love: he was He, my future husband, who happened to be a friend of the agent, He had a cleaning shop in Hollywood for movies stars. His business was booming.

Love becomes an uncontrollable feeling which sweeps you of your feet, incomprehensible in its giving and misunderstood in its taking, long journeys seekers travel to come to meet their destiny to be found in a unique person, that do not have nothing to do with you or your past. Your being awakens to a new reality in life.

The Vision

Yet today I saw a vision that the corona virus was just a face coin, where the other side was our own corruptible sins, and trespasses on ourselves and on others.

We are harvesting the virus with every evil deed we do, and the chickens come to roost, we are being pay what we have done, nothing less.

This 2020, some friend said was a year of vision: but of what vision?

VISION

We are blind by our circumstances since birth. We are born blind, even though we say we can see because we say it, our blindness still remains.

That is what the Gospel of John tells us from the blind man from birth parable.

True Vision is selective and it takes a progressive process to achieve it. Once you achieve vision, you do not see everything in the whole universe. Your Vision is Selective: You can only see God!

But once you see God in everything, you see God working in everything! You see God using bad and good in balancing the Creation.

We are intentionally blinded to many parts of the universe. We are not allowed to see many things or experienced many things. This is why what belongs to the universe is being administered by the Spirit and its power is beyond our comprehension.

The universe is organized in such a way that we are only allowed to see what is designated for us. The universe is focused on a particular singular perception view of the world.

The Mirror of the Mind

This is a broken reality, everyone has a broken piece of glass that they see the world with, yet the mind adapts to this broken piece of reality, and once the mind adopts then believe comes and makes reality whole for that vision of the mind.

The mind is like a bird, flying great distances just to find a niche where to stay, and she finds in a tree of reality, when that tree is shaken, then the nich is moved and the bird has to adapt to another reality.

Then belief comes and the mind becomes unshakable and unmoved. That's when the heart becomes a rock.

The mind mirrors reality, like a swan flying over a lake, mirrors in the lake its flight.

The problem becomes evident in this pandemic: ordinary people do not believe there is a Coronavirus. They believe it is a joke and go around without a mask, gathered in crowds until they get it and it is too late: they complaint: I thought it was a joke, but it is real when in their dying bed realized a little bit to late. Thousands of people die this way.

The reality is that this universe is an overlapping world of things in the present, past and future, but it is unseen by the naked eye. One has to have a better vision to see the unseen things of the world. A third eye of faith, or believe in what is not seen. Your vision will determine the future things that will happen to you.

The more you see. The more it will reveal to you an overlapping realities one on top of another; it is an incredible universe of creations, which surpasses the imagination.

There is a story in Ezekiel that he saw a chariot with many eyes on the wheels and on the body of the

Chariot, which move forward and backwards at the same time; I could not understand why of the many eyes? Now I know that the whole of Creation is being reveal to be perceived by the vision (BEHOLD) we have of the future. Joel prophecy also says: "your old will have dreams and your youth visions!'

THE TRAGEDY OF THE PANDEMIC IS THAT PEOPLE DO NOT HAVE

VISION > TO BEHOLD THE FUTURE. That is being reveal to them by the unseen, world that opens up and its fate is in being blind, there is no greater blindness than the one that does not want to see.

Berkeley was right when he postulate that to be exist is to be perceive, "Vision determines your birth after you are born, And your fate when you cannot see more of a forever revealing universe that only comes alive when you see it. That is how powerful your vision is.

PANDEMIA 2

I woke up and it was a new day never before live.

The old reality vanished before my hands, the pandemic took dear ones, loved ones, und the foundation of what we build our reality.

We start a new reality, making the mind adopt. The new normal appears estranged to us and to the world.

Politics interfered with the need to help: the conservatives wanted to do business in the time of Corona, and only look at the profit side of the crises and not the human toll. They delay to prepare for it because it was bad for business and Wall street. The liberal wanted to help the underdogs of society, giving economic stimulus checks to the workers and not just the corporations. But the corporations and presidents family got the bulk of the money, and everyone was left still wanting and in need.

The mind had to survive had evolved with a new world by creating a new foundation of this new reality, just like a bird building a new nest. This reality mirrors a new and different world.

The pandemic has shift our vision of reality. No longer would be the same again. No longer would we do the same things as before and never again. The mind does not create a new world order, but it adapts to it, by adjusting its vision of this new reality.

It was the death of the old order, and a new birth of the new world, with a different vision on everything. Our logic and reasoning would not be symbolic anymore but of time, space and place.

We would think just like a computer.

PANDEMIA 3

It becomes surreal, like a divorce from reality. Noting seems the same, from New York to L.A.

From North to South, everything has changed. In an unseen manner, which drove the mind insane.

We were so accustomed to seeing things that represent our everyday reality that for centuries we got used to it until this threat, this menace, this unseen virus appears in our imagination with tragic results in our vision.

What we did not see. Shifted our reality, our consciousness and our truth. What was verifiable as truth, did not appear as truth now: our work, our churches, our sports, our commute, our friends, our community, not even our money.

The normalcy was taken away under your feet. You did not have anywhere to stand on your own two feet. The wealth was taken away according to Wall Street. The economy that we were so proud of. From the White House, sound as a witch doctor, or a shaman, or a snake oil vendor, selling false hopes of magical cure for this virus. Inject yourself with sanitizer, etc. becoming a nightmare of all the cures suggested. Cleanse your body with ultra violet rays of light.

I cleanse my body only with the Blood of Jesus, Mr. President.

If you are not pure and cleanse inside, how can you cleanse the outside? Mr. President.

PANDEMIA 4

THE PROPERTY PHILOSOPHER

In the universe, nothing is free but own. In this creation everything that is created is own.

Owners are the ultimate state of being. We are simply property of the higher power. That is why private property is a natural state of mind and of being.

That is why our existence is an indwelling. Higher powers come and indwell in us (Holy Spirit, God, Jesus etc.) We are truly vessels of a higher power. Your existence can never be satisfied until you are filled in yourself. Complete, actualized, fulfilled, and destined to be a star in the heavens above. Own and completed.

We own ourselves, we own the problem or issue that will affect us. We own our suffering that is power of a higher source. We own the world because we become afflicted with so many) sufferings.

We are owners of ourselves, therefore we become Pathos of the ultimate, because our being is being afflicted to the end.

All love is gain thru suffering, all possession is obtain with sacrifice.

Thus our sacrifice, suffering and affliction the universe bestowed upon us the ownership of our life. The world conferred on us the ownership of our death.

You stake your claim upon existence of your property. You are the property owner of time, place and

Matter. You claim for your name everything your experience.

When you realized this, you would own more than the riches man in Wall Street. Your legacy will become a testament and will for the higher powers of heaven. They will write your name in the book of Holy Spirit and when our legacy is done, then they will give you your inheritance and open the testament and there will be your name in the book of life. Don't forget Property Owner to give to God what is due to Him and to you, the angels will bestow upon you what is yours since the beginning of time. So be It.

Joseph Moctezuma Rivera in the time of the Coronavirus. 4-21-2020

PANDEMIA 5

FEAR

We can never be save in any moment of time; that is the message of the virus and the response from a human heart is fear! Naked fear, the unbearable heaviness of fear.

We begin to do everything based on an unconscious fear in our guts. We do not know why, but we are running scare of the stranger, of the unexpected, of the strange and unknown, we become afraid of our shadow.

The most terrible decisions we make is out of fear: we go to war based on fear.

One of the reality of fear is that we kill for fear, like a policeman kills in an instant if she or he believes that his or her life is in danger.

Another reality of fear is that we become blind and do not see anything else but the focus of our fear.

It does not have to be real, as long as it reality to us

In fear, we only see the appearance not the reality behind it. We are threaten, even though there is no reality or threat. Our fears make us live in shadows of appearances, always blinded us to a much beautiful and better reality outside of lust.

PANDEMIA 6

Everything in existence is based on non – existence

Our minds see what is not there, in order to see what is there. It is like Michael Angelo seeing the finished product of his sculptural work in a piece of marmol!

We cannot see the future until we see what is there already. This is the vision of the Pandemic: seeing the future already exist in our minds and hearts to change what is out there. The coronavirus cannot be seen or grasp it returns to the realm of nothing. The mind use non-being for everything.

PANDEMIA 7

Knowledge is a trap, by knowing you become responsible of what you know and you get trapped in what you know and that is what I called Karma.

It is not what you do that gets judge but the knowledge of you doing it what is judge.

So you are trapped in existence because of you knowledge and that brings judgment upon you.

The Indian and Buddhist system of Samsara or the wheel of return and the concept of Nirvana advocated the trapped and liberation of existence.

Jesus advocated that if you want to enter the Kingdom of God, you have to be like a child (devoid of knowing of what going to happen to you).

Even when God created Adam and Eve. He created them in a state of Spontaneous Grace. And forbid them to eat of the tree of knowledge.

So the consequences of knowledge brings Final Judgment of things and of yourself and that judgment creates Hell, Karma and the Wheel of Rebirth, terrible things that tied you to existence forever.

How can you liberate yourself? Don't let yourself know of anything you do in life, do not let the devil know or yourself of your intentions.

The more conscious you become of your deeds, the more you announce it with blow horns to the world! In addition, spirits and dominions will come to see what you are doing.

The Bible says that "do not let the right hand knows what the left hand is doing" and when you pray to God, God will reward you in secret.

Another problem of epistemology is that a soul is loss when it wins the world, in other words "what does it profit a man to win the whole world and lose his only begotten soul?"

Once your soul is loss, who or what will stand in judgement. Have you seen ever a man insane be judge my humans standards? Because once the mind is not conscious, who is guilty or who is responsible or who is accountable?

PANDEMIA 8

The neurosis started, very subtle and inconspicuous it creep on the minds of those that for 6 weeks were cloistered in their homes, trying their best to follow rules on regulations, administered by the authorities. Unbeknown to them the neurosis grew inside of them like an insidious plague more dangerous than the virus outside. COVID 19 affect your body, but Neurosis a state of mind of hyper anxiety and uncertainty hammering the belief that we are never save in any point of our lives. Our focus is on o shifting reality that changes by the hour, leaving us in a panic mode, always walking on the razor edge of time and space not knowing what will present to us next time.

We created a state of normalcy, and believed that it was definite and stable. A stable reality that we can rely on not to our detriment, yet the Pandemia told us that it wasn't the case, and the anger grew in us acting out of tune and making us to crazy things like protesting in house of congress with war gear and assault weapons, demanding our freedom (freedom from the Coronavirus) can we shoot the virus with our guns? A neurosis like a dog in heat, humping water hydruns or legs of humans. Man was not made for an unstable reality in the world. But a certainty of mind that knowledge or knowing can bring you. We are creature with mind and mind is only a compass that tell us that everything is ok by knowing it, confirming as fact and justifying our existence with that Ape of knowledge. Once that confirmation and surety is not given to us, neurosis infect our minds and we start to like an alternative reality suitable to calm us and make us peaceful again.

We have Hollywood in the age of Depression. We have wars when we no longer understand the other or others. We have destruction of ourselves and destruction of everything when we do not understand. Yet the universe is lacking in justification and knowledge because nothing is explained to us and everything has a secret code or genie inside a bottle.

The greatest Neurosis is our computers that works only thru codes secret password and insurmountable number of windows with no self-explanation. No wonder people now a days do weird and bizarre life, estranged from everyone and isolated from the greater humanity, they practice social distancing for fear of the virus.

PANDEMIA 8.5

NEUROSIS

There was a neurosis in society that engulfs everyone whether cognitive or not to joint in a mass neurosis due to the panic und uncertainty of the times. That is why young reasonable and logical men go to war and kills on a professional basis. That is why nativism and hatred of race comes without justification and when brutal and outrageous conduct becomes prevalent in a society that become unconscious with their neurosis.

PANDEMIA 9

We were left with nothing, naked of all activity. Stranded at home with nothing to do. We could not go back to the reality that we have lived for so many years. All activity cease to be in every street corner, in every street and in every city.

God said: "retired to your home, and I will make you new, and give you a different perspective in life." I will make a new reality for you, as long you recognized that there is NOTHING YOU CAN DO IN LIFE WITHOUT ME" thus said the Lord of the highest.

Everything we do is for God. I knew that since the beginning, but we tend to live with ourselves so much that we attributed everything to us, for us and by us. Unconsciously we trying to be god and live in our own terms everything. This is what was wrong with the reality that was broken into pieces by the Corona Virus.

THE DILEMMA

Johnny was not happy staying home. "I feel they (government) have taken my freedom. I feel like a slave, they have taken my constitutional rights and confined me as a prisoner in my home.

The government edict rules and stay at home compliance. All were advice so we can combat the virus. Yet Johnny felt he was imprisoned and wanted to protest this rule to stay at home.

When the president announce that all states were to relax the edict and rules and open business again. The dilemma came haunting him like a spectra in the night.

If I go to work without being tested I could get infected and go to the hospital and be susceptible of dying. But if I stay home and not go to work, I will not have anything to eat and die anyway. But he remember in his Sunday school that was said by Jesus: "which is more important, the dress that you are wearing or the life that was already giving to you?" isn't life more important that the dress? We stay home for life, we go out for the dress that we wear.

PANDEMIA 10

Rufino did not have no identity: no place to belong, to be himself and know himself, he feel he was a stranger to others and a stranger to himself.

He was isolated in high school, only keeping to himself, if it really was a self in him.

He graduated, but did not get his yearbook that he so much desire, he did not go to Disney Land like all his class, but he got his graduation ring that he wore it so proud, because he had accomplished something to his long latter of success.

He went to a local two years college, walking for miles back and forth, just likes he did in high school. His classmates painfully saw him walking and they stop to give him a ride.

He graduated with an AA degree. He immediately went to a four years university to obtain that Bachelor degree that he always wanted. Once he obtained his bachelor degree, he discovered that there was a disparity between his high education and the job market; the job market did not hired Mexican, even though with a bachelor degree.

All what he could get was a paper route early in the morning dropping Los Angeles Times at the doors of neighbors and local neighborhood.

Even his coworkers would asked him why was he doing there with high school dropouts, if he had a college degree? He could not answer them, even after getting his Master degree in Education, could not fine a decent job for his education. That would last his whole life time...

PANDEMIA 11

EXPIRATION DATE

There is a system imposed on us, of hours and days. On all existence. All beings are postdated, for certain time of expiration. Our days and hours are numbered for an expiration date.

Nothing lust in existence offer its expiration date. Within that system we are given a work to do, yet we are not conscious of it, but we do it for a greater meaning and significance that are in the stars and heavens above.

That is the mystery of our existence; that is why we go with the event, the happening and the fate of our lives, our destiny is created beyond our grasp. For our knowledge does not grasp this higher meaning of time.

One of the lessons of this Pandemia is that we all have an expiration date. But what increase our neurosis and anxiety is who hos the expiration day for this Coronavirus and who has not.

PANDEMIA 12

Death becomes a reality hidden behind life in its fullest extent.

It is something you already knew, but was trying to hide in the back of your mind.

It was something that you were acquaintance with like an old friend that you did not see for many years and it show up at your doorsteps, a reality incomprehensible in your existence, but was integral part of it.

In this reality, nothing seems to fit or nobody seems to be prepared.

Like the virus, it hits you and surprises you, you being naked.

Marisela was a friend I knew for many ears.

She carry a great presence in all of us, yet we did not know it at that time.

She was ambitions, blond and devoted to the Catholic rites of devotion.

We celebrated weddings together, funerals and baptisms

She always look up to people of power, but she was interested in what I represented to her.

She was a member of my bible study, always coming to the meetings and living with us the serendipity of moments together.

Then suddenly, she had cancer and the whole world around her changed in a split second.

Not enough time to think why things happened.

It just presented itself on the door step of you comfortable home and shook every bone of your body; no logic, no reason, no cause or effect could justified is presence.

Ambiguous and uncertain. Leaving you one door for escape: INSANITY!